Welcome to The GROW & READ Early Reader Program!

The GROW & READ book program was developed under the supervision of reading specialists to develop kids' reading skills while emphasizing the delight of storytelling. The series was created to help children enjoy learning to read and is perfect for shared reading and reading aloud.

These GROW & READ levels will help you choose the best book for every reader.

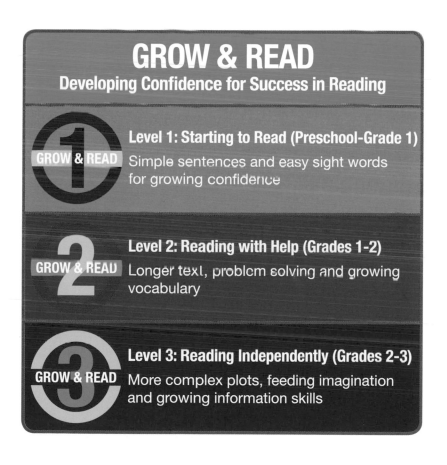

GROW & READ
Developing Confidence for Success in Reading

GROW & READ 1

Level 1: Starting to Read (Preschool-Grade 1)
Simple sentences and easy sight words for growing confidence

GROW & READ 2

Level 2: Reading with Help (Grades 1-2)
Longer text, problem solving and growing vocabulary

GROW & READ 3

Level 3: Reading Independently (Grades 2-3)
More complex plots, feeding imagination and growing information skills

For more information visit growandread.com.

Published by Fabled Films LLC, New York

ISBN: 978-1-944020-19-4

Library of Congress Control Number: 2018944489

First Edition: October 2018

1 3 5 7 9 10 8 6 4 2

Cover Designed by Jaime Mendola-Hobbie
Jacket & Interior Art by Josie Yee
Interior Book Design by Aleks Gulan
Typeset in Stemple Garamond, Mrs. Ant and Pacific Northwest
Printed by Everbest in China

FABLED FILMS PRESS
NEW YORK CITY
fabledfilms.com

For information on bulk purchases for promotional use please contact Consortium Book Sales & Distribution Sales department at ingrampublishersvcs@ingramcontent.com or 1-866-400-5351.

The
Peculiar Possum

by

Tracey Hecht

Illustrations by
Josie Yee

Fabled Films Press
New York

Chapter 1

The stars were twinkling.

The moon was bright.

But a fox, a pangolin, and a sugar glider were wide awake.

They were nocturnal, and it was time for their breakfast.

"Pah!" Bismark exclaimed.

"Where are all my pomelos?

This tree is usually filled with them!

But tonight I can find only one!"

Bismark folded his
sugar glider flaps.

Bismark tapped his
tiny foot.

Bismark scratched the
bald spot on his head.

7

Suddenly, a strange noise
filled the night air.

CLUCK
CLUCK
CLATTER!
CHIT
CHIT
CHATTER!

"Oh goodness," Tobin said.

Tobin scrunched his scaly shoulders.

Tobin clasped his pangolin claws.

"What was that?" Tobin asked.

The fox took a step forward.

The fox's name was Dawn.

"Hello?" Dawn said to the darkness.
"Is someone there?"

CLUCK
CLUCK
CLATTER!
CHIT
CHIT
CHATTER!

The strange noise sounded again!

Chapter 2

"Great gliders!" Bismark gasped.

"First, I cannot find my pomelos.

Then there is a strange chit and chatter.

I know what it is.

We have a prowler in our presence!"

"Oh goodness!" Tobin whispered.
"A prowler?"

"Yes," Bismark said. "A prowler of my
pomelos! A thief!"

Suddenly, the wind blew.

The shadows shifted.

A strange smell filled the air.

Tobin's eyes grew wide.

"That *is* an odd odor," Tobin said.

"I do not know that scent.
Maybe we do have a prowler!"

Dawn raised her head.

She sniffed the air with her snout.

"The smell is coming from up there."
Dawn pointed to the branches of the
pomelo tree.

WHISH!

WHISH!

Above them, the branches parted.

Out popped two shiny, brown eyes.

And a paw, holding a pomelo!

Chapter 3

"Popping peepers!" Bismark bellowed.

"There is the prowler!

And it has one of my precious pomelos!"

WHISH!

The peepers vanished.

The paw and the pomelo disappeared, too.

The branches on the right rustled.

The branches on the left rustled.

And then, out rolled a pomelo!
It plonked right down onto the ground.

"Oh my," Tobin said.

"I think the prowler has returned the pomelo!"

CLUCK CLUCK CLATTER! CHIT CHIT CHATTER!

The branches parted again.

This time, the prowler appeared.

The prowler blinked her big peepers.

The prowler wiggled her pointy ears.

The prowler swung
from the hairless
patch of her tail.

And then, the prowler
plopped right down in
front of them!

Chapter 4

"Moonlight madness!" Bismark declared.

"The prowler is a possum!

And it just **kerplunked** right out of the tree!"

Dawn, Tobin, and Bismark gathered around
the possum.

The possum did not move.

"Pardon me?"
Dawn said to the possum.

But the possum did not answer.

"Perhaps this possum is feeling a bit peaky,"
Dawn said.

Just then, the possum popped open one eye.

"I am not feeling peaky," the possum said.

"I am feeling fine.

I am just playing possum.

That's what we possums do."

Tobin was perplexed.

"Playing possum?" Tobin asked.
"What is that?"

"It is what possums do when we are afraid," the possum said.

"We lay flat and do not move."

"Oh!" Tobin said.

"But you don't need to be afraid.

We were just collecting pomelos."

The possum looked at the three friends.

The possum **CHITTERED!**

The possum **CHATTERED!**

And then the possum popped
up to her feet.

"I am Penny," the possum said.

The possum stuck out her paw.

"Pleased to meet you."

Bismark took a step forward.

Bismark narrowed one eye.

"Well, I am Bismark," Bismark said.

"And I am not pleased to meet you.

Not pleased at all."

Chapter 5

Penny's peepers popped wide.

"But why?" Penny asked.

"I am a pleasant possum."

Bismark put his hands on his hips.

"No, Penny, you are not," Bismark said.

"You are not pleasant.

You are peculiar."

"Bismark," Dawn said.
"That is not polite."

"Well, it's true," Bismark said.

"Penny is peculiar.

Penny prowls and she pillages.

See! Penny has one of my pomelos right there." Bismark pointed.

"Bismark," Dawn said. "These pomelos belong to everyone."

Bismark pouted.

"Well, Penny clucks and Penny clatters.

And she chits and she chatters.

The way Penny hablos is downright

bizarro!"

Dawn raised her eyebrow.

"Bismark, do you know someone else who

speaks bizarro?"

"But," Bismark said, "what about that peculiar patch!"

Bismark pointed to the hairless part of Penny's tail.

Dawn smiled gently.

She looked down at Bismark's bald spot.

"Bismark, Penny is not the only one with a hairless patch."

"Yes, but pee-yew!" Bismark persisted.

"Penny smells different.

And Penny plays dead!

That is plenty peculiar."

"Bismark," Dawn said.

"Playing dead is what possums do
when they are afraid.

It is perfectly normal."

Tobin scurried to Penny's side.

"Penny, I spray a terrible odor when I get scared."

Tobin reached for Penny's paw.

"Bismark," Dawn said.

"None of us are exactly alike.

But that doesn't make us peculiar.

That makes each of us unique."

Penny stepped forward.

"You see, Bismark," Penny said.
"I am not peculiar.
I am simply a possum.

                    And I am proud."

Chapter 6

Bismark sighed.

Bismark harumphed.

But then, Bismark
took a deep breath.

"You are right," Bismark said.

"Penny, I owe you an apology."

Bismark hopped onto a rock.
Bismark raised one arm high.
Bismark bowed low.

"Penny, you are not peculiar.

You are your own possum.

And that makes you perfect."

Penny smiled.

Penny puffed up with pride.

It was a superb apology!

Bismark picked up the pomelo.

"Penny," Bismark said, would you like to share this pomelo?"

Penny smiled. Penny nodded 'yes'.

"Perfecto!" Bismark said.

"We will have a pomelo picnic!"

"And there is nothing peculiar about that!"

The NoCTURNALS
FUN FACTS!

What are The Nocturnal Animals?

Pangolin: The pangolin is covered with keratin scales on most of its body except its belly and face. Pangolins spray a stinky odor, much like a skunk, to ward off danger. It then curls into a ball to protect against attack. Pangolins have long, sticky tongues to eat ants and termites. Pangolins do not have teeth.

Red Fox: The red fox has reddish fur with a big bushy tail and a white tip. Red foxes are clever creatures with keen eyesight. They have large, upright ears to hear sounds far away.

Sugar Glider: The sugar glider is a small marsupial. It looks like a flying squirrel. It has short gray fur and black rings around its big eyes. It has a black stripe that runs from its nose to the end of its tail. Sugar gliders have special skin that stretches from the ankle to the wrist. This special skin allows sugar gliders to glide from tree to tree to find food and escape danger.

Brushtail Possum: The brushtail possum is one of the largest tree dwelling marsupials. They have a pointed face, long oval ears, pink nose, and bushy tail. They spend their days asleep in their nest and feed on plants at night. They rely on sight, hearing, touch, smell, and taste to move around in the forest.

Nighttime Fun Facts!

Pomelos are fruits much like grapefruits. They are the Nocturnal Brigade's favorite food to eat. They have yellow or light green peels and pink citrusy flesh. They are the biggest citrus fruits in the world!

Nocturnal animals are animals that are awake and active at night. They sleep during the day.

Language Glossary

Bizarre

(bih-zahr) *adjective*
very strange, weird, or unusual

Perfect

(pur-fikt) *adjective*
having no mistakes; so good that it can't be better

Proud

(proud) *adjective*
very happy with yourself or others

Speak

(speek) *verb*
to talk or to say something

Unique

(yoo-neek) *adjective*
not like anything or anyone else

Language Glossary

	Bizarre	Perfect	Proud	Speak	Unique
Arabic	غريب (gha-reeb)	في احسن الاحوال (fi-ahsan-al-ahwal)	فخور (fahk-our)	أتكلم (a-tak-ka-lam)	فريد (fah-reed)
French	bizarre (bee-zar)	parfait (par-fay)	fière (fee-air)	je parle (zhe-parl)	unique (oo-neck)
Mandarin	奇异的 (chee-yee-duh)	完美 (wan-may)	骄傲 (jow-ow)	我说 (wo-shwo)	独特 (doo-tuh)
Portuguese	bizarro (bee-zah-ho)	perfeito (per-fay-too)	orgulhoso (our-gul-ozo)	eu falo (eeu-fahlo)	único (ouni-kou)
Spanish	raro (rah-row)	perfecto (pur-fect-oh)	orgulloso (or-gew-yo-soh)	yo hablo (yo ah-blow)	único (ew-knee-coh)

Be proud to be unique! Look up other languages at
growandread.com or at your local library.

About the Author

Tracey Hecht is a writer and entrepreneur who has written, directed and produced for film. She created a Nocturnals Read Aloud Writing Program in partnership with the New York Public Library that has expanded nationwide. Tracey splits her time between Oquossoc, Maine and New York City.

About the Illustrator

Josie Yee is an award-winning illustrator and graphic artist specializing in children's publishing. She received her BFA from Arizona State University and studied Illustration at the Academy of Art University in San Francisco. She lives in New York City with her daughter, Ana, and their cat, Dude.

About Fabled Films

Fabled Films is a publishing and entertainment company creating original content for young readers and middle grade audiences. Fabled Films Press combines strong literary properties with high quality production values to connect books with generations of parents and their children. Each property is supported with additional content in the form of animated web series and social media as well as websites featuring activities for children, parents, bookstores, educators and librarians.

fabledfilms.com

FABLED FILMS PRESS
New York City

Read All of The Grow & Read Nocturnal Brigade Adventures!

This series can help children enjoy learning to read and is perfect for shared reading and reading aloud.

Great For Kids
Ages 5-7

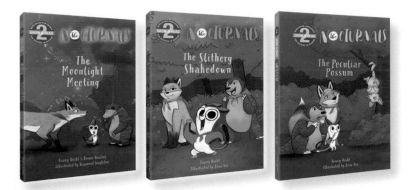

Visit nocturnalsworld.com to
watch animated videos, download fun nighttime
crafts, word games and science projects; or
listen to author Tracey Hecht read the books aloud.

Teachers and Librarians visit growandread.com to download
educational materials and storytime activities.

www.nocturnalsworld.com
#NocturnalsWorld